For Sebastian
K.H.

For Alexander, Jessica and Joel
J.E.

First published 1992
by Walker Books Ltd, 87 Vauxhall Walk
London SE11 5HJ

Text © 1992 Kathy Henderson
Illustrations © 1992 Jennifer Eachus

First printed 1992
Printed and bound in Hong Kong by
South China Printing Co. (1988) Ltd

British Library Cataloguing in Publication Data
Henderson, Kathy
In the middle of the night.
I. Title   II. Eachus, Jennifer
823'.914 [J]

ISBN 0-7445-1540-8

IN THE MIDDLE OF THE NIGHT

Written by
Kathy Henderson

Illustrated by
Jennifer Eachus

WALKER BOOKS
LONDON

A long time after bedtime
when it's very very late
when even dogs dream
and there's deep sleep
breathing through the house

when the doors are locked
and the curtains drawn
and the shops are dark
and the last train's gone
and there's no more traffic in the street
because everyone's asleep

then

the window-cleaner comes
to the high-street shop fronts
and shines at the glass
in the street-lit dark

and a dust-cart rumbles past
on its way to the dump
loaded with the last
of the old day's rubbish.

On the twentieth floor
of the office-block
there's a lighted window
and high up there
another night cleaner's
vacuuming the floor
working nights on her own
while her children sleep at home.

And down in the dome of the observatory
the astronomer who's waited all day for the dark
is watching the good black sky at last
for stars and moons
and spikes of light
through her telescope
in the middle of the night
while everybody sleeps.

At the bakery
the bakers in their floury clothes
mix dough in machines
for tomorrow's loaves of bread

and out by the gate
rows of parked vans wait
for their drivers to come
and take the newly-baked
bread to the shops
for the time when the
bread-eaters wake.

Across the town at the hospital
where the nurses watch in the dim-lit wards
someone very old shuts their eyes
and dies
breathes their very last breath
on their very last night.

Yet not far away on another floor
after months of waiting
a new baby's born
and the mother and the father
hold the baby and smile
and the baby looks up
and the world's just begun

but still everybody sleeps.

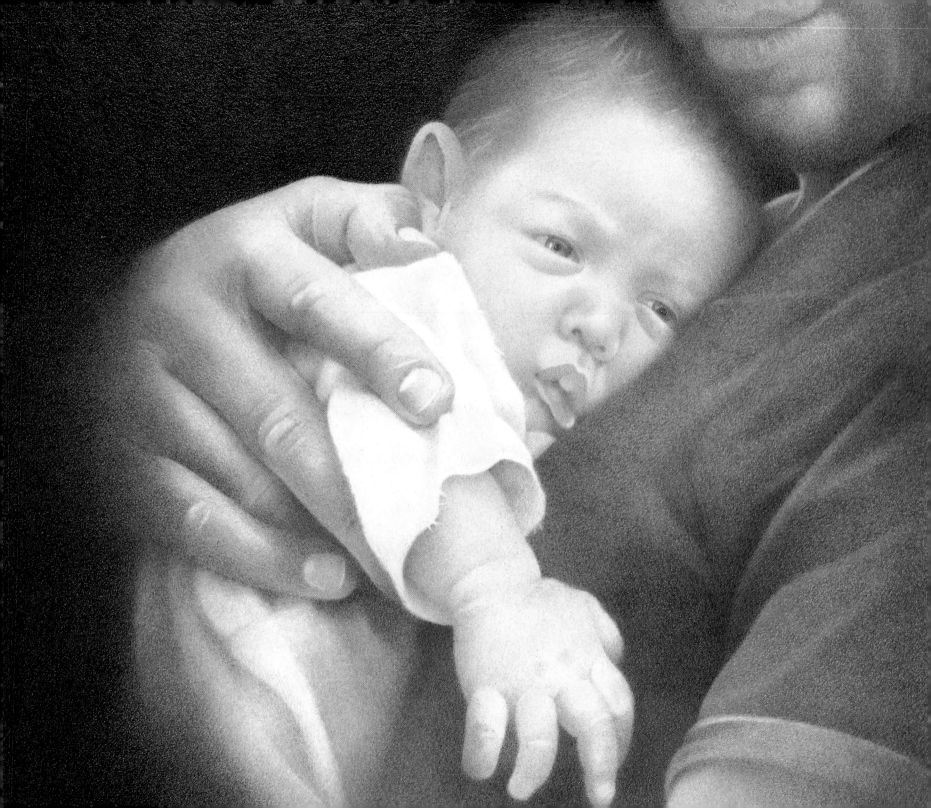

Now through the silent station
past the empty shops
and the office-blocks
past the sleeping streets
and the hospital
a train with no windows
goes rattling by

and inside the train the sorters sift
urgent letters and packets on the late night-shift
so tomorrow's post will arrive in time
at the towns and the villages down the line.

And the mother
with the wakeful child in her arms
walking up and down
and up and down
and up and down
the room
hears the train as it passes by
and the cats by the bins
and the night owl's flight
and hums hushabye and hushabye
we should be asleep now
you and I
it's late and time to close your eyes

it's the middle of the night.